A Poetic Walk th

Volume

Index of Poems:

Arthurs Seat
Mynydd Maen
Match Day
Ebbw vale
West Mon Pontypool
Elwy and Taff and the Fierce Tiger
Not Evil but Holy
Tuesday Night training
Cardigan Bay Cardigan days
Shields Bright and Gleaming
The Lion of Trellech
Brychan Loves Llansoy
Front of the river Blaenafon
On the slopes of the Black mountains
Mari Llwyd Maesteg Mari Llwyd
Bargoed Canvas
Afan Parc Wonder
Island of Cynfaeth
Llanfihangel Crucornau Courthouse
Pop into Pandy
Adorable Cwnyou
Frances and Daisy
For the love of wool
Beautiful Builth Wells
Gwarafog Bridge
Pisttyll Rhaedr
Claerwen Walley
Montgomery, Montgomery

Passing By
Y Trallwng This sinking land
Newtown, Hometown, Freetown
Llanfair Caereinion Picture Book
Cyfronydd Revealed
Hug the lonely tree of Llanfyllin
The Old Barn café
Llanhaedrym Mochnant
Meirionnydd's Legacy
Llangollen's Voice
Wrecsam, Wrexham, a Kings court indeed
All attention on Leeswood
The Slopes of Bryn Alyn
Slashing Ice
Can you take me to Wepre Park
Nercwys Fair Tower
Ffynnon Leinw
Edwards Iron Ring – Flint Castle
St Winefrides Well
Ysceifiog
Rhes-Y-Cae Show
Caerwys in Bloom
Telacres Blue Moon
Bodelwyddan Peace
Kinmel Bay
Llanfair Talhairns Black Lion
Nantglyn
Ffestiniog's Promise
Twrog's Boulder
Llyn Mair's Sweet Echoe
Rhyd
Fanny Edwards writes from Penrhyndeudraeth
Bryn Bwbach
Eisingrug Pond
Storiel and Pontio Bangor's Beating Heart
Bangor Mountain
Our Menai Bridge
Oriel Tegfrn
Llanfaes – Once Capital of Gwynedd
In Llandonna a Hidden Gem

Cestyll Garden
Historic and Prehistoric Mynydd Carningli
Hen Galen
Mighty Cwmbran
Mynydd –Y-Garth, Gwaelod-Y-Garth

1. Arthur's Seat

Craggy rocks green nimble grass

Waving steadily in the wind

Blowing so hard across this Devonian Outcrop

Whirling winds and ghosts throw down on Cefn Coed

A cold apparition and turns the heads of those in Bwlch

Twisting, gutting between the terraces of Cathedine

Crisp and brisk over the roofs of Llangattock

Harsh biting cold chilling Llanthony

A raw beauty, a bleak Wonder

A beautiful valley

A Mountainous paradise

This graded highland that passes on

This unseen majesty that embraces our souls

And within this kingdom stands a king

Where Arthur sits and rests

This is its head, the head of the Dragon

Warriors still run on Pen Y Fan

They pride their might on its test

Hoping to be Arthur's best

Com Du is his twin

Walks, Charity runs and Special Forces

Snow Mist rain and Ice

A forbidding seat to endure, bronze aged graves still adhere

The cold brisk wind pushes again

Pushing the ghosts of ancients kings

Rolling Highland and biting wind

The Mountains Peak, the Beacons Summit

Beds of sandstone dip slowly gently southward

Now our Legendary Kings play again with fun and laughter's promise

Chasing and playing with Tommy Jones upon that Holy Summit

And in the wind on top of the Beacon Tommy jones is free to giggle

Rested at peace with all our kings

On a clear day you can see the World, and still here Tommy play

2. Mynydd Maen

Walking up past Cromwell's end

To the steps where Tony descends

Up on the road turning left and then east

Up the rise to the bridge with a name for this place

There he is majestic in glory

My great rock mountain with tumbling stone

Overlooking the valley like a king from the past

Green and ragged where Torfaen once dreamed

The breaking of rocks, and rock breakers once famed

And now forward still to the village of home

Of places of people who once I ran too

Now different but the same the people grow fonder

A centre a metropolis, an urban beginning

This village a city with pubs and curries

To the right shall we go to Wellers domain

Of years playing army and tags with old friends

Or right to a street named after a chapel

To a girl I once dated who lived in Caer-yr-Ebol

No forward I think up that trapper's hill

Trapping my heart as it beats I wonder for long

Hello and Hello's to Ashley on Friday nights

Bouncy castles and fun, and way too much pop

Time with Ashley I'll never forget

Up further the rise gets steeper to a church with a steeple

A welsh village like no other a canal needs cleaning it's full of Algae

And now near the top I look left to nan and bamps

Leo and Vera say hello from the past

Roll ups and wrestling I'll never forget

As nan shouts at the tele "get Giant Haystacks"

A now a rim of the old trappas hill looking down and the streets where a mayor roams

Looking up he looks back my great Mynydd Maen

A Palisade of Hope a mount of abundance

That sows goodness into this Eastern Valley

Puffing and Panting I've not yet begun

But decide to just look at the palace above

I stand the longest time in awe for a human

That loves this place but travelled still further

My heart is here with my great mountain

Torfaen is the home where great things do start

3. Match day

Getting ready after breakfast the whole family

Anticipation deepens who's got the tickets

The train leaves in 30 we'll get a taxi down

Red the colour of day

Red shirts Red scarf's painted faces

Symbols of old a dragons face

Pendragon's army alive once again

Bundled in the taxi drives, a distance we could have walked

In the air the Valley breathes, as we arrive at the station

Excitement in the air, energy in the conversations

High Spirits, big dreams of anticipation

A packed platform with more still arriving

A waiting room of patients who need a prescription

A train approaching we get ready to embark

Crowded carriages full of fun and laughter

Now a sea of red and scarfs and children

And men of age with every reason

Now on to Cardiff to watch Wales play

It's our weekend holiday it's our match day

4. Ebbw Vale

A crisp green morning brings the fox close to home

Rolling hills and valleys enjoys springs bloom

Clouds dance across the sky, enjoying their fresh waltz against the canopy of light

Green hills, lush pasture, craggy rock

The rock pushes through the sullen earth

Children racing down the hills jumping from rock to rock

Still wet from the wanted wind

The rain drifts lightly now gone

The giddiness of childhood, a clapping between stones

Children's laughter on the steep valley rise

Ebbw Vale below encouraging the future

Deep holes filled in new hopes being built

Restored for tomorrow and Children's laughter

The signs of spring continue

Steelworks no more but now vigor

New hopes, ideas, placed on a new path

Growing again, growing again

The sun peaks through the darkest of clouds

Warms the faces of the children who play

Nye Skips down Western Terrace

Enjoying the day of pleasure

Of lighter hearts and clearer eyes

The future looks brighter for all who travel

On Ebbw's path, which now looks wider

5. West Mon Pontypool

(Dedicated to the teachers of West Monmouthshire School past and present)

Walking up Crane Street all full of bluster

Of fluster of hoping this time will pass

Ideas and thoughts and chasings of lily

Welsh valley wanderings in hill sides and mountains

Ysgol Gorllewin *Mynwy it wasn't back then*

Just West Mon a school for boys to be kings

From this place many were started some ended

But Anthony just passing

Just passing through this Welsh Valleys times

With sounds of work, of peace and hope

Singing it seems down Pontypool's grey Streets

Preaching is heard at its corners

Gwyneth Jones sings her songs in the highest possible pitch

Seth Joshua preaches on a box made of wood

A dancing spirit throughout the town

A toughest place, a place of peace

Ebdon kicks the ball against the wall

Scoring once again, through many times Anthony walks Towards his West Mon School

Time is mixing this early morn, with Pontypool past and present

Children's voices miners swearing

When looking back and looking forward so much to hope for

Walking in the Italian Gardens thinking of the future

Anthony think's he'd like to act, like in the flix

"I don't belong here I need to move on"

"I feel like a lion in Winter"..

But Pontypool won't forget this friend who passes by some times

1949 with hope and fury

An ended war a new beginning

Of people who haven't been born yet

That will push Pontypool forward from and blessed past.

And West Mon a cornerstone of change

Now young men and young woman

Shaping a future together

Achieving Believing Succeeding

6. Elwy and Taff and the Fierce Tiger

Big Taff and Little Taff start their beautiful song

Pure and free like the Beacons they do meander

A bright flow of freshness, moving south

Playfully hoping to the place of end

Of a place where waters gather

Now onto that spring that Thermal Well

Tumbling along now southeast we go

Radyr, Whitchurch, Llandaff, Pontcanna

And then to Grangetown, to the Tiger's Liar

Meeting with Elwy to open her mouth

From Tonyrefail flowing South

Sunlight piercing her Holy water

And on brim of Elwy's bow

Laughter and song can be found

Tumbling onwards boulders tumble

Towards Tiger Bay its depths do rumble

Now meeting Taff in warm embrace

A Native brook, has now become

The Tiger's Bay a vicious tide

Children play from all over

From every nation it seems to wander

To plant a home among these docks

And play together without concern

Birthed from this mix she takes a drink

From this bay to quench her first

"Don't drink that it's full of coal!"

A sister shouts and Points a finger

Birthed from this place she likes to sing

A mixed family like a blended Scotch!

A Holy voice though sisters don't agree

"Shut Up" is all that Shirley here's

Singing strong too strong for some

Soulful, hopeful, joyful

Shirley's voice becomes a hum

Of one day soon of national pride

But as for now a stage is set at Mooreland's School

Of Splotts big future still yet to tell

Running home from Tiger Bay

Shirley sings out again

A voice that carries hope

So strong that it becomes a guiding post

So strong that Taff sings back

And Elwy smiles and begins to clap

Of two great rivers who became one face

This is the beginning of a wondrous place

7. Not Evil But Holy

(Dedicated to the memory of Rev Thomas Price, Welsh Language defendant, Aberdare)

Thomas walks a winter tail

Of old saying and wrong tongues

To which he is known to all in this parish

Not lazy or immoral

Not weak or evil

Winter's cold brings sharpness of mind

Of prayer and hope as to whom designed

"Is this language I speak such evil?"

A language so old, so warm in its whistle

But not just a Baptist's cause, a nation's cause

Maybe even further a Holy Cause

Who is to say who is right and who is wrong?

Or that a language is Holy or Evil

God in his temple decides such things

Not mere men who now run to Merthyr

To debate is best to consider these things

Here in Aberdare still free

The way we speak the words we use

The valley echo's each pronounced verb with vigor

Debates they ran in Capel Calfaria

In rooms of town halls, whether night or day

Aberdare is here to stay with fortunes now changing

Iron and coal forging forward to man's employ

Industry and enterprise fills the air

Thomas Powell opens a fourth pit and the town now changes

With schools and chapels full, Aberdare now centred

Walking down Cardiff Street Thomas breaks a smile

"A Holy language it is then, and forward for Aberdare"

8. Tuesday night training

Dropping and falling splashing and pouring

Clouds break with heaviness of rain

Swirling winds and cold frigid tearing

Across each chosen hill and valley

In the darkness glints of light

A union of placed pitch

Tuesday night training and with rugby as its God

Cold skin muddied thighs and the smell of oil and grease

Drills, practice forwards lining out

Filthy shirts and soaked brows and bandages around

A ruck is formed, shouts cry out forwards push towards the prize

Scrum down, tight 5 have won that prize again

Hero's and warriors every one

Those backs stay clean they're pretty boys waiting on the wing

Waiting for those fighting forwards to pass that golden ball

The works been done all they have to do is run

The rain continues to fall

And of course they drop the ball and complain about the weather

Forwards sigh and start again

9. Cardigan Bay, Cardigan day's

An Indent in the coast of Wales

Welcoming the fresh breeze and the torrents of the Irish Sea

Cardigan Bay, Bae Ceredigion

A Marine paradise, drifting, shifting, forgetting

Ever moving, ever staying

An Ancient forest beneath the waves

Grey Seals ponder, on rocky shores

Enjoying the warm west sun

Sea plunges and caps, cubs run and swim

Rain drops, sea drops and mist

Refreshing, revitalizing, Cardigan's hope

The Tempest Whisks those curling waves

Bottlenose Dolphins jump ahead

Playing underneath the Mistral Wind

God's most beautiful place

Marine and Terra in harmony

Children flock to see the dolphins

Happiness, giddiness and excitement

Parents remember it takes them back

To be a child again full of wonder

Spirits rest, souls refreshed in Cardigan Bay

Youthfulness returns

They are young again

As the breeze, breathes and flutters

Blows away the hurts the pains the tough days. Only in Cardigan Bay

Seaside resorts, Cold Ice cream, Fish and Chips

Warm sunshine, cool water, waves to jump over

Sir Gwaun meets the sea in Fishguard

Pirates and Frenchmen and the last great Invasion

Borth stands aside an ancient forest, submerged beneath the sea

A golden sandy beach where Granny drinks tea

A place of peace, Cantrf Gwaelod a sunken kingdom, A Welsh Atlantis

A hidden past that says hello sometimes

Through storms and lower tides

Aberystwyth, mouth of the Ystwyth

Capital of Mid Wales, that old Uni town

A railway that hangs from a cliff

Victorian Architecture, Gothic feelings embrace a classic revival

Meadows and Forests as old as the hills

A pier, a promenade so much fun to be had

A Welsh God of war now rest on the quay

Aberayron nestles in in the frost of Aeron's valley

A warm glow in summertime, steep beaches and pebbles

The best place in the World for Honey Ice cream

Eating softly sitting on the Quay, enjoying the blue flag beach

Welsh ponies and cobs in the warm summer breeze

And a Carnival Queens procession to Alban's fair Square

Onward our journey with friends we all share

Through blust and blister in the mid day sun,

The heat it grows with most to differ

On now to a place where Neptune came

And leave behind his ancient pain

On Llangrannog beach he left his tooth

So no more the pain he felt once left

Today when walking on Llangrannog's shore

You'll see what's left of Bica's snag

And singing Welsh in modern tone

The Urdd's children have now come home

Fun pools and rock pools at Llanon beach

Sea cliff's recede from the attack of the sea

Pools to fish made by monks from the past

Lots of great fishing the saint's mother does cast

A different place on that same coast

Shipbuilding its roots and now something different

Holiday makers amass mainly from the midlands

Part of the Snowdonia beautiful range

A tourist attraction has birthed a new place

Aberdyfi stands strong in this Cardigan Bay

From past it captures a Spanish interest

A bear from Amsterdam came stuck in its entrance

Copper was mined to help Welsh princes

Old forts destroyed on Pen-y-Bryn hill

A beautiful beach, glisten in the sunset

Warmth in a glow of fun and health

Children paddle in cool waters

Waves roll in tossing buckets aside

Building Castles sanded to the shore

Parents rest, laid back in the sun

In profusion abounding in peace

A lifeboat drifts by as pictures are taken

No rescue today calm water reside

And on a quiet day when the waves are so quiet

Bells can be heard beneath the water

Still ringing from lost kingdoms life

Cantre'r Gwaelod beneath, and beneath remain

Wander past in deep seclusion

Cwmtydu missed but worth the visit

A cave a kiln and seals sleep

On Cwmtydu's hidden shore

Now a basin of salt this town finds its name

Given its Charter through a Black prince

And the market still stands on every Wednesday

Pwllheli that beautiful town

A place to relax and wind down

For generations memories were made

In the echo of "Butlins" Starcoast World

Where soldiers once marched children did pass

And infants with parents enjoyed amusement arcades

3 legged spoon races, that lasted decades

Boisterous fun for everyone

Under Pwllhelli's sun

Enjoyable memories now continue

As holidays are booked and enjoyments with the zest of entertainment

But just a small part of Pwllheli we've visited

So much more to this town

Albert walks up Pen-Y-Garn

Which stirs his hope in poetic charm

Cynan smiles a breath of hope

An understanding of how man's soul is found

From this salt basin a poet did rise

In statue in grace disarming Welsh pride

Disarming indeed was all that he wrote for

The rigors of war still plaguing his mettle

To an Unknown God he wrote his poetry

And God did listen and blessed him immeasurably

Now walking down to catch the bus

Away to Bangor to watch the game

A rugby match "I should write about that"

Now we keep walking through Cardigan Bay

There's a few other places that come our way

So many places we've missed on our tour

Places that glean of silver and gold

Where the people make the coldest hearts glow

Come now and visit Cardigan Bay

Rest a little while and stay for the day

10. Shields Bright and Gleaming

Marching in lavish green fields

Armour and Swords Clanking

Dripping wet from the fresh morn dew

The sun burns through, gleams of the bronze

So far from Rome a new home found

The dull sound of soldier's boots

Trampling on the bosky callow

Treading the grass of a Welsh Hillside

Walking now towards the town

Of rest from weary conscripts

From Isca have they travelled

Back home now among the generous people

Liberal Abundance avoided by home

Carleon's seen just over a hill

A bath should be taken to reduce weary limbs

And tonight enjoy the music in the Amphitheatre's cool night

Carleon a base so much more

Nestled in a valley gloating Rome's Glory

Isca Augusta a fortress of types

Legio II Augusta brings peace to the night

Away from the darkness comes Rome's pure light

Now down to the Harbour and fish on the Wysg

Fresh Fish for supper

A soldier must eat

11. The Lion of Trellech

Walking down Wye Valley way

Enjoying the day with warm sun shining

Come across a public house

Well Established and still standing

A Coaching House, A pig farm but now so much more

The Lion Inn Trellech's sweet ancient core

Taste buds love you then you ponder

The great tasting Ales that are on offer

Malty Biscuity grainy and rich

The Ale certainly helps scratch that itch

Deep roasty smokey and sweet

The Lion Inn Ale is quite the treat

Rusty layered piney and earthy

We don't deserve this we're not worthy

Zippy fresh bright and sharp

We're so glad we walked on Trellech's Path

Herbal Spring like aromatic and floral

Thank you for Ale we all sing in Chorus

With Open fires and wooden beams adorning a splendour

Take a visit to Trellech, you might stay there forever

12. Brychan Loves Llansoy

Go East said Brychan Go east and settle

Those pleasant hills those lush valley floors where good food grows

From Ireland we came and married a wife

Garthmadrun was fun

Older now he tells his descendants

My sons go east, and find a new place

Settle in the valley

And enjoy peace forevermore

Brcyeiniog is my home but yours is another

Llansoy they settled in a sweet morning dream

Near Raglan's sweet charm

A beautiful valley and a wonderful brook

From Sweet waters we drink

God's place we all think

Dyfrig is young and helps us build homes

Llansoy Llansoy we've only begun

13. Front of the River Blaenafon

Coal

It mined

It mined from here

And so much more

The Source of the Afon Lwyd

Flowing Down

Abersychan, Pontnewynedd, Pontypool, Llanfrechfa and Cwmbran

Flowing down

Upstream Blaenafon sits

Iron works was its start blast furnaces around

Iron workers from Stafford came to settle

Samuel Hopkins, father to the town in extravagance

And Sarah Hopkins built the school

Stack Square workers rest

Viaducts become homes

Samuel tries to learn the name of every worker

1804 Samuel and Thomas Build a church

Truly settled now

Flowing down front of the river

Ty-Mawr Hopkins hope becomes a hospital

Serving again

A Legacy, vandalized

And Now a family home again

And Now a Book Town

And Now the Big Pit

And Now Industrial Heritage

And Now Amazing Blaenafon

And Now a new Beginning

And now an incredible future……

14. On The Slopes of the Black Mountain

The River flows through the town

Starting from the Black Mountains

Together Y Mynydd Du, Afon Wysg

Abounding in fish, flowing deeply through

A progressive course

Ebbs effusion and flows

A flood of plenty

Riddling and running

Estuaries and mudflats

Saltmarsh and Lagoons

Grasslands and woodlands

Stemming down, moving forward

The river Usk continues its course

A river of legend, of stories to bet

Where Gwain pushes Arthur into the Usk

Then has to explain to Guinevere why he's come home so wet

Britons then Romans then Normans fished here

All delighted with the mass of catch

Now on a day when you have some spare time

And you feel healthy and relaxed and sublime

There is a route called the Usk Valley walk

From Carleon it follows the course of the river

Joining Uskmouth just up a little further

Passing Roman Carleon which is such a treat

Then Climbing up Wentwood to a steep ridge

The descending gently in pastures and fields

Continues it does to Usk and Y-Fenni

Welcoming the Beacons in all of their glory

It follows the towpath along the canal

Climbing upwards just after Llangynidr

With Fine views of mountains majestic above

And from a forest rejoining at Penecelli

The Route ends at Brecon and it's time for a rest

The flowing river, the gaining hope

Do enjoy your time

On the Usk River

15. Mari Lwyd Maesteg Mari Lwyd

The night is cold

The threat of snow

Men sing and shout

With Happiness and song they are denied entry

No you cannot come in, sing the patrons

Much to the men's laughter and singing

Let us is, another Sings

Mari Lwyd hold that skull high

Hold that Skull high and let us enter its Christmas in Maesteg

Bells ring and the sackcloth robed men dance

Ribbons of all colours blow in the Cool December wind

A riddling contest, a singing contest the only way in is to win

Mari Lwyd cast out, from a stable in Bethlehem on a cold night

So many years ago, now finding a new place to give birth to her colt

Let us in Let us in

It's Christmas in Maesteg

16. Bargoed's Canvas

Like a dash of paint

Art can lift you towards greater things

Waiting for the touch of a masters hand

A boulder, A scrag of rock

Lush Green valley

Swift and swipe of the artists brush

Creating new what was seen old

Like an old sentinel it stands there

Over the pit head the colliery's depth

A stroke of the brush, ah glancing of hues

Paint drips

The Canvas begins its story

Of a place in the Valley

Of a place where men worked

Toiled and ground in sweat

An Aqueduct, a hillside

Bargoed's broken past

Laurence, changes the pallet

Fresh Colour added

Industrial heartland

Men at work at the pitside

Men at work in the cavaness depth of the earth

Lowry breaths out the smell of industry he breathes in

A lush green valley, a hopeful place

Bargoed on canvas a miner's image

Finishing he smiles in a considered manner

This is not the end for this coal side town

The sun shines and children sing poem

A great future still awaits

For all who call Bargoed home

17. Afan Parc Wonder

Great Summer fun, walking breathing feeling

Lungs delight under heavens blessed sight

Steep sided valley's eyes delight

Quite lonely bliss hearing natures depth

Solitude a reverence

The new bird sings

Another trail examines, the need for fun and rich

Mountain bikes throw up clumps of mud and fun

The Wall Trail opens…with fast stream ragged climbs

Paradise for bikes

Penhydd trail 22 kms of ride for life

The trail you ride before you die

Down Hill down White level

It's the speed that you'll love

Stunning views from the horizon line, South Wales is alive

Forest sprawl out, mountains push up

Natures palace looms

Enjoyment abounds and blooms

The sun sets after a furious day

All are tired from the play

At Afan Forest Park

18. Island of Cynfaeth

A noble place remembered by time

A village so quiet as people do chime

Church Bells still toil at the passing of hope

Such a beautiful place it helped Stephen cope

A pretty little church with a long history

A heavy and austere exterior a simple unspoilt interior

St Bridget would be proud that so many explore

Just across from those hallowed door

Ynysgynwwraidd so little known

Skenfrith a little more

A ruined Castle for all to explore

A fun place to pretend

A broken fort next to the river

Which the Normans built after 1066

To protect from the "Welsh" those barbarous bunch!

One of three castles, that defended the area

The Lordship of King Stephen was quiet daring

To clear the road from England to Wales

Skenfrith a wondrous place

And sometimes forgotten

But well worth the visit

To say hi to Bridget

19. Llanfihangel Crucornau Courthouse

Laying on the Eastern edge

The village still splendours

A pint of beer please at Wales oldest Inn

Owain Glyndwr rallied his forces

While enjoying a pint of the local brew

Some say it isn't the oldest but we say it is

Now enjoying a drink on some cold winter night

Listen carefully to what you here

In the wind whispers ghosts still wander

Times past in the Vale of Ewyas some folks were into sheep stealing

Tough back then but still a crime

And a place was needed to try them

The Skirrid Inn became that place

And even the place to hang them

But enjoy your lunch forget those tales

We didn't mean to frighten

But just in case you here some noises

Don't be worried

Just have another whiskey

20. Pop into Pandy

One mile from a border

One mile not so far

Beautiful Rolling green Hills

Rolling from Afar

Clear skies warm hearts

A village full of Wonder

Walking down past Ty-Newydd Farm

The air is fresh and living

The locals are warm and welcoming

On past the post office walking no further

Lungs filled with hope and hearts filled with laughter

Can any place be better?

Pack now to a home cooked breakfast

The Lancaster arms is calling

21. Adorable Cymyou

A captivating little place

On the slopes of Hatterrall Hill

An Ambrosial Hamlet

A much loved place to visit

A Hillwalkers delight

The warm sun so bright

Appealing and attractive

Visitors amass up bryn and mountain

Walking Gospel Pass

A heavenly breeze pleasing to feel

Runs down from the valley over Hatterall Hill

Walking up towards St Martins

Perched high on a hill

A very serene and tranquil place

And one the prettiest places you've seen

The light is ambient with hope

We can see Capel-y-Ffin

Glimmering is the distance

Looking around standing on a steep hillside on the east side of the valley

Occasionally subject to slippage

Like the rest of us

The Chancel weeps but best of all

All the stones are indeed turning

A happy and delightful spot

The preciousness of this valley is beyond price

The sun spills into the church

Through a leaded Tudor window

The Black Mountains laying beyond

Nothing could be so utterly Welsh

Buried in these stones is Britain's cultural gene

A sonnet played out in a landscape

A radiant place touched by God

An alluring beckoning

When you leave, you'll want to come back

Wherever you are Cymiou's Sonata plays

Clear skies, green valleys

An attractive darling in a Welsh Hillside

Fascinating pleasing and refreshing

Come visit

Come visit Cymyou

22. Frances and Daisy

Llanigon is such a pretty place

Ebbeded in lovers romance

A changing tale is now here

Of what was once a tragedy

Walking across Llanthomas bridge

The morning early rising

Frances walks over the water

Deep in though and heart wondering

Will she marry or will she not

Not even a pound to my name

Will Rev Thomas look down on me

Even though I may still prosper

Walking now on Ash Grove sweet Daisy did appear

A fragrance drifting with appealing

And hope for Frances future

With drift and hope his knee was bent

And looks up to her that made him

Sweet Daisy Marry me and all what's mine is yours

I'll take you and the pound that all you have

Don't even bother asking dad

He's a miserable old Pastor

And so they were married this happy love

And forever they held each other

Llanigon's new Pastor's

23. For the Love of Wool

Blankets throws and ties

Scarfs hats and Fabric

Historical weaving in Wales

And a space suit made of wool

Afon Irfan flows gently

With Mynydd Epynt above

700 years of weaving wonders

Fabric dyed carded woven and spun

Royal wool woven here

Queens and Princes felt it's warmth

Cambrian Woolen Mill still producing

The Heart of Wales passes through

Bog Snorkeling, man versus horse

Dol-Y Coed Hotel with new electrons

Going places…..

Hotels built for spas

A small town with a massive heart

Llanwrtyd Wells still amazing

24. Beautiful Builth Wells

Lying at the confluence of the Wye

A pristine place that will never tire

With Llanelwedd as its friend

St Mary's Church in Bualit

Llanfair-ym-Mualit

From Past Vortigern lived here

Inviting Saxon's to his pasture

Cwrt Llechrhyd still shines

Llewelyn washes his head

Ambushed maybe but never dead

A ford across the Wye

A flowing hope for all to enjoy

As a lawyer writes

The Mabinogion is finished

A market town still grows

The Royal Welsh still shimmers

Now walking down Garth Road

A sound is heard

A spirit rises

A song is sung and the soul is fired

From the Greyhound voices ring

Echoes of melody no longer dim

Lyric and poem in the air

Drifting verse and aria

Men they sing those pure Welsh songs

A ballad a chant for all to here

A call a Chorus that brings a hope

An anthem a chanson

A piece and line

Comrades in song singing just fine

Builth Male voice choir

Arranging a Sonnet

Llewelyn walks past away from the mire

David sits on his white rock

Myfanwy to admire

Cwm Rhondda sang out

To the pull of piano wire

No darkness here

A light has acquired

In Built's streets alive and inspired

25. Gwarafog Bridge

An ordinary day graced by water

On a bridge, Gwarafog bridge

Casting out hunting for fish

The ebb and flow of Irfon

Lit by the moon

Serenity embraces life

Lights from Garth glow the distance love

Beneath the cool moons light

Friends cast and share

Stars sparkle fair

Above Powys beautiful and still

Rest for the weary

Smiles among friends

Melting darkness innocent waters

Brightened dreams Irfon's streams

Forever friends and laughter

26. Pistyll Rhaeadr

Tumbling down, falling fast

Cascading down Pistyll Raeadr

Falling smashing plunging down from ancient rock

An Iron bridge

Woodland walks and footpaths

A teaching place

A flood of spirit rushing down

A gush a plunge, forever now

A torrent of legend

An outpouring of myth

And a deluge of truth

The spoils of Annwn

Berwyns, a mythical place of past

Giants monsters and magicians

Mathonwy showers her children at the base of the falls

Manawyddan Bran and Bronwyn

The children of light

Playing in the sunshine

Through a waters Holy mist

A channel of happiness

A place of peace

Warm sun, soft sky

The land of ancient Britons

Sprinkling water

Irrigates the soul

A drenched spirit underneath the falls

An overflow of hope

Saturates the mind

The water of Rhea

Love between giants

Faces still seen in the rock

Stay a while

At the foot of the falls

Breathe deep

Clear mind

An unmistakeable freedom

At Pistyll Rheadr

27. Claerwen Valley

Unmistakable beauty lies in these hills

The Mountains a great splendour

Distinct and plain in creation's heart

Fresh and clean is the air

Rugged hillsides

Mountain dew

Brooks falling steeply

A Walkers paradise

In Elan and Claerwen valley

Stream and waterfalls

Filling up the basin

Drifting shallows wondrous depths

In all considered hallowed

A walk around that reservoir

So peaceful, so peaceful

28. Montgomery Montgomery

Montgomery Montgomery

You're a beautiful town

Warmed from the Sun

Not even a frown

Down Broad Street we walk

Straight into checkers

For cheddar we crave and Dan wants sweet Peppers

Such wonderful food, such a wonderful place

With some lovely aftertastes

Filled and happy we continue our journey

Say hi to Doris, Miss Evans and Bernie

Drifting past the flower house

Sweet smells and aroma's to the music of Straus

Crossing the street near the Ivy house café

Friends say hi we no longer dismay

Montgomery is our home it's a wonderful town

So beautiful it could be wearing a crown

Up the Hill on Church Bank

At the Top of the hill we say hi to Frank

This place these people so warming it is

So happy we are it's like we won a quiz

Now here we are the place that we see

Over the Bowls the hills they do gleam

If you get the chance you should visit Montgomery

Honestly, it will feel like you've won the lottery

29. Passing by…

A483 and passing by

Ffron so pretty a little happy place

Smoke of logs burning in the air

Mossy wet valley that we love to adore

A telephone box

An old water pump

And a view of the Severn

30. Y Trallwng – This sinking land

This marshy sinking land

A glimpse of solid fortune

Georgian Architecture blooms it's streets

A warm wind

A welcoming breeze

Greets all it meets

Home to Welsh Princes

Saints alike in grandeur

Llewelyn and Cynvelyn called it home

A sandstone castle overlooking the Severn

Red walls and terraced gardens

And enjoyable sight for all

Steam trains tussle by

Lovers and children smile

Narrow lanes and Cattle Markets

A wonderful place to be

Montgomery canal and Offa's Dyke

Walkers and barges paradise

Wonderful Welshpool

The people so warm

So giving and pleasant in this Powis town

Visit this place

Maybe stay a while

Relax and resemble

Y Trallwng is on the rise

31. Newtown, Home town, Freetown

Harry Beadles shoots and scores

John Bentley fights for Wisconsin

Geraint Goodwin writes his short story

Barry Hoban cycles past on his way to France

George Lanthan heads the ball

Robert Owen believes in a better world

Phillip Parkin places his Tee deeply in the ground, and gets ready to swing

Pryce Pryce-Jones licks the envelope and has an idea and sings

Phil Mills goes left left left as the mud flies behind

Thomas Powell feels radical it's time to lead the blind

So many people

So many faces

Hero's all some you know and some you don't

What's the secret to this Welsh Manor

So many successes

So many raising the banner

A Newtown A Hope Town

A place for tomorrow

It's people keep pushing to go further and faster

It all begins with the way they teach

It all begins with how they're taught

Ysgol Cedewain stands out from the crowd

Where beautiful inclusion is allowed

The Student's so bright their achievement so wonderful

Their minds and hearts incredibly so colourful

So rich in beauty

And deeply intelligent

The way they are taught is nothing but excellent

Ladywell Green school

What a wonderful place

Singing and dancing creating and laughing

Toddlers they run and giggle in the morning

By afternoon they have eaten and some begin yawning

A great local school for kids to be part of

A great start to life you can feel the love

Hafren Juniors

Filled with bright futures

Encouraging Children to reach full potential

The things they'll achieve will become monumental

Each student the chance to be successful

Ysgol Dafydd Llywd

Where the red dragon stands

Creating amazing things with their hands

Welsh language flows and named after a poet

Dafydd would be proud of the intelligence that is flowing

St Mary's promoting well being and freedom

These student's will never be beaten

The light of intelligence

Shines bright like a beacon

Penyglodffa A vibrant hopeful place

With hardwork and inspiration the students do create

A wonderful future for themselves and indeed others

Working together like sisters and brothers

No task too hard no challenge too hard

Penyglodffa primary the future explored

Maesyrhandir Schhol what a fabulous School

Where Eco and Eisteddfod are in the same pool

Where everybody is somebody

Mae Pawb Yn Rhywun

The students are learning abundantly

Treowen is vibrant fun filled with laughter

With learning and education that last forever after

Where children are taught to be the best they can be

Where hearts and minds are indeed set free

Newtown High School Last but not Least

Forever bold and encouraging

Forever bright and successful

The students hardworking and respectful

The grades impressive the work eventful

Delivering students full of potential

The school is packed full with clubs and activities

Pushing hope and greatness and reducing negativity

It's schools like these raising Newtown's brave Banner

Putting this great town on the map

And bringing Wales great Answers

Newtown Newtown

This is the place where we'll settle

Where teachers are so great they deserves a medal

In Montgomeryshire's heart

Picturesque and beautiful

Barnwy valley surrounds its peace

A quaint and sleep exterior

A picture book feel

A typical traditional Welsh town

Hilly street and Barnwy bridge

St Mary's stands

In Llanfair's heart

On the banks of the Barnwy

An idyllic place to wander

The past rushes by

As the water continues its journey

Drift and lose yourself at Llanfair Caereinion

Lose yourself and enjoy your day

33. Cyfronydd Revealed

The wind deep the valley aches

Rain pours the slopes do fill

A storm in Powys

The lightening does flash

The sky parts the sun shines

And heaven is revealed

Wind deep

And Cyfronydd is revealed

A pasture so wonderful

The dew so beautiful

And Cyfronydd is revealed

34. Hug the Lonely Tree of Llanfyllin

Drifting now it's past a glory

Hugged enough too old it's time

A tree hugged for hope for life and prayer

To work together together to end despair

The tree now done its legacy

To hug each other instead of trees

Then on Sunday go to Pendref and say thanks

To the God of all who made his entrance

Hug your friends where the tree once stood

Say a Prayer in Pendraf's home

And success will follow all your days

Think in that chapel of all your dreams

And today is the time that heaven remains

35. The Old Barn Café

The old barn café

Tucked into Vyrnwy's pleasant valley

With a Dam good view

With a lake for pleasure

Llanwydd around and luscious

Simon's Giant hand

Pushing up open to the heavens

A nature reserve

A paradise of wildlife

Heather Moreland settled around the lake

Fresh bread, fine teas and clotted cream

Good times good company

Sugar with my tea

A friendly welcome

A hillside walk

Deep breathes inhaled

Peace to the soul

Freedom to the mind

Cycle hire and fun

At the Old Barn café

36. Llanrhaedrym Mochnant

Quiet and traditional

Beautiful and biblical

Nestling in a small valley

Blessing the villagers gladly

A footpath leads down into the town

Luscious green hills all around

Park street ahead Cottages so idyllic

Down towards the Hand

The sunrise Angelic

Past the post office on Market Street

Across from Keegan's

The best kind of meats

Now up the Street where waterfall's run

A steep little rise towards the sun

A warmth of glow

In this heavenly place

Llanrhaedrym Mochnant

Natures embrace

37. Meirionnydd's Legacy

Standing on the banks of the Dee

Beneath the Berwyn Mountains

Ruthin one way

Llangollen the other

The true Prince of Wales

Crowned in Glyndyfrdwy

Mounted on his battle horse

Overlooking Corwen's square

Overlooking Wales

And it's interests

Encouraging the Youth of Corwen's future

Proudly stand

And be our leaders

38. Llangollen's Voice

A voice in the wind calls home from the heart

Drifting Melodies, sung with the harp

Echoing hills and river's flow

Llangollen's voice a beautiful mellow

Laughter and beauty fill it's air

Culture and prose to adore

A bridge spanning over the Dee

Carries the echoes of the past

A sword of old battles, the crown of a prince

Welsh hearts are full

Bones full of vigor

A carrying verse makes the world so much bigger

A song from the heart in pavilion departs

Lifting the souls of all who depart

Lungs full of air with voices most tender

Hymn's focused only toward heaven

Holiday makers cross the seventh wonder

The Wild pheasant and the Gales of Llangollen

The Dee rapids under

Kayaks compete against the water

Saint Collen founds the church

Dinas Bran ready to fight

Steam trains and whistles fill the air

The rushing water

So close to hear

Pebbles tumble

As we cross the bridge

Fresh air and Welsh hope touch the skin

Towering mountains

Surrounding the voice

Built by the voice

Alive because of the voice

Brown Dee tumbling under

Dee side Café

A walk along the river

Porters to buy Cheese and whiskey

Llangollen's voice is wondrous and beautiful

Touching every accent and nation

A fabric of Welshness

That causes a freedom

39. Wrecsam Wrexham A Kings court indeed

Drifting mist

Wandering over this wishful town

A city really bold in Character

Between the Welsh Mountains

And the lower Dee valley

Sits a North Wallian Gem

So much offering

So much past

So much future

A guided history

So little known

Romans settled in Plas Coch

Celtic speaking inhabitants and English Invaders

Mercian Colonists on the River Gwenfro

Giving Wrexham her name

A native Welsh Lordship called Maelor

Wrexham a house of Powys Fadog

Madoc ap Gruffydd Maelor smiles

Sees God in the Mist

And Valle Crucis is built

After Llewelyn on to Marcher

Villa Mercatoria

Our beautiful market town

Royalists and Parliament fight it out

Then onwards some forward to Wrecsam town

Iron Mad Wilkinson opens in Bersham

Now Industry is here

And turner paints a water colour

This town is a city

A city is this town

Some complain that it's not good enough

But the truth remains it's better than good enough

It's delightful and incredible

And full of potential

It's people important and very successful

A city with hope for all its children

A future bright and ever so blissful

Wonderful villages become

Like moons around the planet

Llan-y-Pwll so lovely and bright

Marford and Gresford sweet homes delight

Llay a coal mining village of past

Where men and woman worked and crafted

Alyn Waters Country park

With a sister parc in Gwersllyt

Forest's and footpaths

Carved wooden animals

Pleasant air hopeful future

In Alyn Country Parc

Gwersyllt densely packed village

A Welsh campsite

A pint in the Wheatsheaf

A railway station takes you anywhere

Rodney and Rosemary walking together

Off to Church looking up and seeing hope

One daughter close the other a bit further

Bradley and the Old Mill Estate

Brynteg and the castle Inn

Brymbo and Harwd

A steel works now gone

But new hope does muster

Industrial Archaeology everywhere

Wonderful people

Wonderful parks

And Cheshire View

Where the past was discovered

Our beautiful burnt wood in Coedpoeth

And Saint Tudfil finds her home

A chapel of ease

Coal mines and lead mines

A wonderful village

Where Andrew donated a Library

Made of local sandstone

Where Gwenfron stood at the pulpit

And preached heaven's wonders

Rock place with a wonderful view of the Cheshire plain

Bersham and Rhostyllen

Side by side

Rhosllanerchrugog still Welsh speaking

Heath of the heather glade

Beibi a rhaw I bobl y Rhos

Coal mines and chapels

Heritage and culture alive and well

Singing fills the air

Cor Meibion Rhosllanerchrugog

Cor Orffiws y Rhos, Cor pensiynwyr

Cor Merched, cantorion Rhos

Wherever you go singing

Marchwiel, Standing strong

Always standing strong

Saint Marcella so beautiful

Ysgol Deinol an amazing school

Berwyn Drive so peaceful at night

And a little shout out to Minera and Gwynfrn

Lovely communities

Wrexham so proud

With a Giant killer team

Wrexham so incredible

Wrexham so amazing

Wrexham so strong

40. All Attention on Leeswood

No Welsh can be spoken

No Welsh at all

This mine is owned by the English Man

No Welsh allowed

Coed llai did wake up

And a riot did take place

A change of hearts and minds

Allowed Welsh to be spoken freely again

41. The slopes of Bryn Alyn

Lovely Llanferres

Upper Valley of the River Alyn

On the eastern slopes of the Clwydian Hills

Just south of Moel Famau

A place of incredible natural beauty

Offa's Dyke trailing by

Caer Gwyn and Ty n-Llan

So pleasant to come home to

A place we'd call home

A place for hearts to be rescued

42. Slashing Ice

Cutting across the ice

Energy pushing down

The cold can bite

So much fun

She moves like a dream

A jump a toe loop

The onlooker's hoop

She builds up speed

And feels the invigorated air

Sliding, slicing turning

Gliding effortlessly

To onlookers delight

The atmosphere positive and vibrant

A waltz jump

Then a loop jump

The background music pumps

She moves like a song

Every Saturday she'll be here

Deeside Ice rink

So cool and friendly

Where skaters come to enjoy the company

43. Can you take me to Wepre Park

Flintshire's Gem

Planted next to an ancient forest

Warmed by the sun

Fed by the rain

Wepre Park

To be enjoyed again and again

Rich in wildlife and history

Water and Hill

Gwy and Bre

A little arched bridge

Allows the mind to wander

Of Victorian days

And now so much fonder

Old halls and water falls

And a Guardian in the woods

Red rocks and Birch trees

All at Wepre Park

44. Nercwys Fair Tower

The Terrig trickles downward slope

Gently passing the eastern fringe of the Clwydians

A medieval passing over by

The Tower still stands

Fortified and strong

Still bearing the scars of border tussles

The Tower still Fair

A home still warm

The Tower stands in Nercwys camp

Gothic revivals and medieval fortunes

Without God there is nothing

Heb dduw heb ddim

Twr Broncoed inspiring poets past and present

45. Ffynnon Leinw

Flowing tides

Water hides

It's healthy spiritual side

A drinking well

A blessed place

Gaining youthfulness and vigor

Drinking cool and fresh from well

Enjoy the purist splendour

Rhydymwyn Ffynnon Leinw

You might just live forever

46. Edwards Iron Ring – Flint Castle

Edwards Iron Ring

With Hope to sift

Flint's gem adrift

On the Dee's ebbing flow

The fortress ablaze

Burned to protect Edwards's forces

In the wrong hands Dafydd ap Gruffyd

Would change the balance of power in the region

Welsh forces would never be beaten

A constable starts the blaze for the hero's

For Edwards name and all his arrows

Later repaired and partly rebuilt

Welsh hopes remain and persist

Welsh dreams unfold

A nation is built

Changed by conflicted the castle is silted

Beautiful today for all who visit

In Peace Mr Turner came

With a canvas and paint with his own flame

A water colour now lives free

In Flintshire's dream

Worth a visit we guarantee

47. St Winefride's Well

The water's of Life

A sad tale began

A rose did grow where she lay

Innocent the blood of fair maiden

Raised to life at the Green Chapel

Now legacy of life to all that visit

A miraculous cure in those waters

Winefride's gift to all who pass

Quenched the thirst of Sir Gawain

To fight a green night

Who he overcame

The Lourdes of Wales

Many amazing tales

Of Miracles and chivalry

Richard the I

And Henry the V

Travelling there by foot

Deep cool healing waters

Refresh a broken soul

Pearl patience and purity

Healing minds and bringing clarity

A place of peace

To lose yourself

A place of hope

To find yourself

48. Ysceifiog

Green fields and pasture

Sweet summer breezes drift smells and aroma's

Lazy summer days

Elder trees and warm meadows

Sitting outside the Fox Inn

Enjoying the Summer eve

Ysceifog has it made

It's the place of our dreams

49. Rhes-Y-Cae Show

So much more than a row of fields

So much more than a parish village

Rhes-y-cae show

What a marvelous delight

Dog racing and show jumping

It's quite the sight

Sheepdog trials

The tension is tight

Next time you're travelling through Wales

Spend time at the Rhes-y- Cae show

It's a tremendous delight

50. Caerwys in Bloom

An abundance of flowers and hanging baskets

African daisy's and Alyssum

Aster's with a batchelors button

Bellflower's and Bergernia

Bluebells and Blazing stars

Buttercups and heather

Honeysuckle and Mallows

Cascaded around the town

Main streets and side streets

Caerwys is in bloom

Bringing pleasure to the residents

Bring delight to the visitors

Such a wonderful place

A place to visit

The soul will never prohibit

51. Telacre's Blue Moon

The coolest night

The bluest moon

Shining down of Telacre's sandy dunes

From here the past was strewn

On these night's

Far in the distance

A shape a figure in existence

From the Lighthouse

Out in the water

A figure walks so much closer

A Ghostly past, walks to it's future

The lighthouse keeper walks with a stupor

Walking on Telacre's dunes

Back towards the lighthouse doomed

52. Bodelwyddan Peace

Walking down Maes Owen

We can feel Bodelwyddan's Peace

The rigors of the day

Now gently appeased

Behind us the sweet pasture

That helps our minds to breath

Sixty listed building

Now call this place home

We have found our place here

There's nowhere left to roam

53. Kinmel Bay

Waves slowly crashing into the shore

The rippling swell bouncing the rocks and pebbles

The influx and crest dances over children playing

Jumping over the waves one by one

The water ripples and corkscrews as children laugh and giggle

The tide heaves and flows as the family enjoys the sea

The wind is gentle blushing over the pebbled beach

A friendly tempest of healing sea air

The pleasant sun warms the beach and shore

A summery snug glow fills the Bay

A great day of fun in Kinmel Bay

54. Llanfair Talhairn 's Black Lion

An ancient Three arched bridge

Spanning over the Elwy

An ancient road

To an Ancient place

Leading to the heart of the village

Mynydd Bodran

Overlooking the village

The Black Lion Pub

Our destination

A warm and welcoming place

Real Ale and great food

Llanfair Talhairn's best kept secret

55. Nantglyn

Nantglyn will rise again

Making Wales proud

It's people it's persons

Will hope again, and challenge will be found

Nantglyn, Nantglyn will rise again

And find a new discovery

Nantgyn never small

Will find its new recovery

56. Ffestiniog's Promise

The cool northern wind blows over Pant Llwyd

Ffestiniog below gleaning in the sun

Cwm Teigl in the distance

Surrounded by beauty

Aiko and Shinya

Walk hand in hand over the rugged Welsh Mountains

So far from Takarazuka

So close to home

Like an unseen Majesty the Mountains drift toward eminence

A Mass of palisade capturing their dreams

The valley of luxury is Ffestiniog's hope

Shinya thinks of Nagano and feels at home

Lush green mountains and hillsides

Each breath a treat

Headlands of joy

Air fills their lungs

Standing on this Welsh Mountain

Momona's promise fulfilled

Wales Forever

Cymru am Byth

57. Trwog's Boulder

Rising in the hills of Ffestiniog

Draining from Moelwyn Mawr

Arfon Dwryd passes by

Passing beautiful Maentwrog

Twrog A giant in the village

Unhappy with the pagan Alter

Picks a huge boulder from the hillside

And hurls it high in the sky

With a fierce smash the alter destroyed

Now stands a church

Trwog planted Yew trees

To rest from the sun

He now stays in Maentrwog

Forever now on

58. Llyn Mair's Sweet Echo

Built for Mary

Echo's off the hills

A lovely lake

In Gwynedd's heart

Ancient Oak woods

Fresh air and country walks

Plas Tan-y-Blwch warms with light

A tranquil appearance

A great picnic site

Worth a visit

Worth a stay

59. Rhyd

Incredible Views

Views to take your breath away

Moelwyns Bach

Just stand here and breathe

Breathe deep and take it all in

Surrounded by beauty

Woodlands and Forests

Mountains and Hills

Standing in Rhyd

Just taking it in

60. Fanny Edwards writes from Penrhyndeudraeth

Fanny is fully aware

That the Welsh language has begun to tear

She has to do something and something she does

She picks up pen and paper and creates such a buzz

Children stories she begins to write

Writing in Welsh she brings a bright light

To the minds of children she brings hope and peace

To the Welsh language she brings an increase

Now children in Welsh are telling their stories

Of a nation reborn for hope and new glories

So thank you Fanny for planting that seed

You've helped an entire nation begin to succeed

61. Bryn Bwbach

Great Views of the countryside

Peaceful and serene

Llyn Tecwyn Isaf shimmers in brilliant light

A hill walker's paradise

Even in the rain the hillside a beautiful

62. Eisingrug Pond

If you stand over Eisingrug Pond

On a night full moon

On a night so bright

And in that pond a reflection you see

Of yourself much younger and all that can be

The a long life you'll live and a long life to ponder

Your reflection in Einsingrug pond

Will grant you your wishes

63. Storiel and Pontio Bangor's Beating Heart

Forming the City's Cultural heart

Becoming Bangor's sweetheart

Showing off Welsh talent and arts

Setting Bangor apart

Wonderful Welsh art and exhibitions

Glowing hearts full of Celtic ambitions

Gwynedd's history and a Roman sword

Arts and music so wonderfully adored

Tranquil and enjoyable

Worth a visit by all

64. Bangor Mountain

Rearing up above Bangor

Rocky outcrops and high spots

Guardian over Bangor's hope

Beautiful views of Mennai and Beaumaris

Clothed with trees and beauty

A natural castle in the Welsh heartland

An unseen majesty casts shadows over the city

Gorse mixed woods and grassland

Walk the trail, walk the mountain

Enjoyed at Bangor Mountain

65. Our Menai Bridge

Standing on our Menai bridge

Overlooking our mother

Sweet Ynys Mon

The wind plays peacefully over the straight

Waves tumble into Carreg Yr Halen in the distance

A warm breeze on a summer's day brings us home

Salty air fills our lungs

Peace engraved on Ynys Mon

Looking west to find light

Our Menai Bridge Our sweet delight

66. Oriel Tegfrn

A charming local Gallery

North Wales Leading artists

Poised with individuality

Wonderful art

Displaying Anglesey's heart

In all its wonder and charm

67. Llanfaes Once capital of Gwynedd

Llanfaes sometime Llanmaes

Llan Ffagan Fach

A capital once preserved in beauty

A battle still rages in her past

Wooden forts and Vikings

Peaceful now acquainted to

Llanfaes a riddle of what future will bring

68. In Llandonna a hidden gem

A steep narrow road

Departs Llandonna

And there in front of us

A priceless gem

A beautiful beach

That so seldom do find

The hordes of visitors

That spoil other kinds

Well worth the trip

Well worth the visit

A warm tidal breeze brings us to home

Spectacular golden sands

Clear breathless waters

Porpoises and dolphins

Swim carelessly off shore

A natural spacious haven

A serene peace that fills the soul

You'll never want to leave

69. Cestyll Garden

Rugged Land

Outcrop near the sea

Blowing wind of the Irish Sea

Violet loves the land

See's promise in the ruggedness

Transformed now

With colour and beauty

White Rhododendrons bristle in the breeze

Japanese Maple mingles with yellow witch hazel

Grassy banks with lavender and laburnham

Cafnan flows to the sea

Ynys Mon's little paradise

Situated by the sea

70. Historic and Prehistoric Mynydd Carningli

An iron Age hill fort

So much to ponder

Scree Slopes and rock cliffs

Complex and wonderful

Dominating the countryside

With Newport in it's view

And the coast as it's garden

Defences and entrances

Did Romans Demolish?

Mynydd Carningli a mystery

For time to consider

Pembrokeshire's beauty for all to enjoy

Saint Brynach climbs the mountains

And talks to Angels

Today climb here and enjoy Pembroke's Peace

Camp here tonight and here Angels speak

71. Hen Galan

River Gwaun Rises

In those old Preseii Hills

The Valley full of trees

Oak Beech Alder Willow Rowan and Ash

A gem a diamond within Pembrokeshire

13th of January

Hen Galan is upon us

Children sing Welsh songs

Sweets and Money Callineg

Knocking on doors

School is ignored

Ysgol Llanychllwydog is empty

And the teachers are OK with that

Laughing in the streets

Peacefulness in the home

A chance to begin again

A chance to forget our wrongs

When children are allowed to sing

Good things happen

72. Mighty Cwmbran

Lying within the historic boundaries of Monmouthshire

Now the heart of the Rock Breaker Torfaen

Crows fly over Mynydd Maen

A rain shadow a beautiful mountain

Great walks, great view, great scenery

Mynydd Maen overlooking the Bran

Like a Mighty Welsh soldier

A lush green reminder

Of everything Welsh

A valley carved by toil

Now enjoyed with Splendour

A town united with villages

At first Old Cwmbran, Pontnewydd

Croesyceiliog, Llantarnam, Llanyrafon

Bringing together one people

A new time was started

A New Town created

Monmouthshire Canal still meanders through

Each village a gem

Optimism flows through its streets

Leaders are born in Cwmbran

Leading Wales on

So much potential in Mighty Cwmbran

73. Mynydd Y Garth Gwaelod Y Garth

(Dedicated to June Cunningham)

The Garth

Overlooking Pentrych

Overlooking Cardiff

On a sunny day you can see the world

Taff valley in full radiance

Lush green hillsides

And wondrous views

Walking to the Trig Point

Helps fill the lungs

With fresh Welsh air

Steep track and muddy woods

Meadows full of wild flowers

And Ancient trees all around

Garth Mountain looms over you

Broadleaf woodlands of Ash and Birch

Y Brenin Llywd Haunts the old mine

The King of the Mist can be heard at night

Ffynnon Gruffydd bubbles

And brings healing to some

The Garth filled with Bracken and ferns

With spectacular sweeping views

June wanders down the Garth

On her way to Chapel

From here From the Garth

Anything is possible

I hope you enjoyed A Poetic Walk Through Wales – Volume One. My name is Nic Cunningham, I am a Novice Poet. Thank you for allowing me to express my love for Wales through verse. I was born and raised in the South Wales Valleys and now live in Canada, but all our family still lives in Wales and we visit home regularly.

*POETIC LISCENCE: In researching material for this book I used a variety of sources to assist me in developing verse. You'll note from the poems that often, folklore, mythology and historical figures and places are mentioned, poetic licence has been used to breathe new life and meaning into some of these stories.

I am in the process of writing A Poetic Walk Through Wales Volume – Two. If you would like to have you town of village written about do feel free to contact and connect with me, and tell me about your love for where you live. cwmbranpoet@yahoo.com

Acknowledgments:

The Welsh Assembly Government, Ministers and there staff have been very helpful in connecting me local historical societies and libraries so I could conduct research for this project. Thank you to each one of you.

A Big thank you to my wife Karen and Son Ben who have given me the patience to write this book, a thank you also to my Mam and Dad…who have always encouraged me to write.

Printed in Great Britain
by Amazon